DOUGAL'S SCOTTISH HOLIDAY

'There can be few TV performers who give as
much pleasure as Eric Thompson to viewers
(or shall we say listeners) of all ages. Long may
he and Dougal flourish.'

John Holmstrom in the *New Statesman*

Eric Thompson

DOUGAL'S
Scottish holiday

Based on stories of The Magic Roundabout *by Serge Danot*

Book designed and illustrated by
David Barnett

 KNIGHT BOOKS

the paperback division of Brockhampton Press

Also available
THE ADVENTURES OF DOUGAL

ISBN O 340 15544 2

First published in the UK 1971 by Knight Books,
the paperback division of Brockhampton Press Ltd, Leicester
Third impression 1971

© Librairie Hachette 1969 as *Pollux et le Sapin de Noel*
English text copyright © 1971 Eric Thompson
Illustrations copyright © 1971 Brockhampton Press Ltd

The characters in these stories which appear in the
television films were originally created by
Serge Danot for ORTF in a series entitled
Le Manège Enchanté

Printed and bound in Great Britain by
C. Nicholls & Company Ltd, Manchester

Contents

It is decided

One morning, Dougal woke up very slowly.
First he opened one eye – then he opened the
other; then he closed the first eye and tried
using just one; then he closed the second eye
and started all over again by opening both
very wide and very suddenly.

It was a terrible shock, so he closed them
and went back to sleep.

Come into the garden, Maud,
For the black bat night has flown . . .

sang a voice, very loudly and not very
tunefully. It was Brian.

Come into the garden, Fred,
For the black bat night has fled . . .

he sang, louder than ever and very close to
Dougal's ear. Dougal sat up with a start.

'What!' he screeched. 'What! What! What!'

Come into the garden, Ron,
For the black bat night has gone!

sang Brian, going over to the stove and
putting the kettle on.

Dougal watched him from the bed coldly.

'Have you gone out of your mind completely?' he said.

'Good morning, good morning, good morning!' shouted Brian.

Dougal got out of bed and went very close to Brian.

'You've come very close to me,' said Brian, nervously.

Dougal looked at him *very* hard and then spoke *very* slowly and *very* quietly.

'Mollusc,' he said, 'listen carefully. In the first place you have woken me up. In the second place you are making a great deal of noise. In the third place it's the middle of the night and in the fourth place what are you doing in my place?' He paused.

'Take your time and answer slowly,' he said.

'I get the feeling you're displeased with me,' said Brian, cheerfully. 'Am I right?'

Dougal made some tea.

'Just answer the question,' he said.

'Ah!' said Brian. 'Yes! Ah, yes! Of course! You don't know, do you?'

'Know what?' said Dougal, icily.

'No, of course you wouldn't know!' said Brian. 'How could you?! Silly of me!'

Dougal waited.

'Ha! Ha!' laughed Brian. 'I am a potty old thing! What must you think of me?'

'Do you really want to know?' said Dougal.

'Ha! Ha!' laughed Brian again, just a little nervously. 'Ha! Ha! Ha!'

He took a sip of tea and a deep breath.

'You're taking us all on holiday this winter,' he said, very quickly.

Dougal dropped his cup on the floor.

'You've dropped your cup, old mate,' said Brian.

'*What* did you say?' said Dougal.

'I said you've dropped your cup,' said Brian.

'Before that,' said Dougal.

'Before that?' said Brian. 'Ah! Now you're asking me to remember. Before that . . . hmm . . . what did I say?'

'Yes, what?' said Dougal.

'Ooh, difficult to remember,' said Brian. 'Difficult to make the old brain tick over.'

'Force yourself,' said Dougal.

'Er . . . was it about winter?' said Brian.

'Yes,' said Dougal.

'And a holiday?' said Brian.

'Yes,' said Dougal.

'About winter and a holiday?' said Brian.

'Yes,' said Dougal.

'Could it have been about you taking us all on holiday this winter?' said Brian.

Dougal dropped his saucer.

'You've dropped your saucer, old thing,' said Brian.

'I KNOW!!' screeched Dougal. 'I KNOW!! I KNOW!! *I KNOW*!!' And he picked up the cup and saucer, dropped them again, kicked them across the room and jumped on to a chair.

'I KNOW!!'

'Well, that's all right then if you *know*,' said Brian. 'Can I have another cup of tea?'

Dougal sat down heavily.

'Pour me one,' he said, 'and tell me the worst.'

'Well,' said Brian, 'we thought it would be lovely to have a winter holiday this year and as you're so good at organising things we thought you would make all the arrangements and take us.'

'Who's we?' said Dougal.

'Florence and me,' said Brian, ' . . . and Mr Rusty and Mr MacHenry.'

'Anyone else?' said Dougal.

'Dylan,' said Brian.

'And?' said Dougal.

'Ermintrude,' said Brian.

Dougal groaned.

'What have I done to deserve it?' he said.

Brian finished his tea.

'Well, that's all settled then,' he said. 'I can leave the arrangements to you . . . all right?'

'No, it's not all right!' said Dougal.

'Where are you taking us?' said Brian, brightly.

'Give me time to *think*,' said Dougal, ' . . . per-lease!!'

'Of course,' said Brian. 'I'll get the others

and we'll come back in . . . what? Ten
minutes?'

'Make it three days,' said Dougal, 'and not
a minute sooner.'

'They're very impatient to start,' said
Brian.

'Then tell them to start,' said Dougal. '*I*
shan't mind.'

'Without you?' said Brian. 'Our leader,
our friend and holiday arranger . . .'

'Get out!' said Dougal.

'Any tea left?' said Brian

'GET OUT!!' said Dougal, and Brian
got out.

Dougal sat down and thought. He thought it was rotten of everyone to expect him to arrange their holidays. He thought that a holiday, however, might be rather nice, especially in the winter. So he thought about what sort of holiday it should be.

'Winter,' he mused. 'Where can you go in the winter? It's so *cold* . . .'

He stopped.

'Snow?' he thought. 'That's it! A holiday with snow.' He rushed about.

'What a great notion! And the very place? *Scotland*! Plenty of snow! I'll take them to my Uncle Hamish in Glen Dougal and introduce them to the clan! With any luck I may lose the lot of them in a drift.'

He chortled and ran round in a circle nine times.

'*Scotland the Brave*,' he sang. 'Now where are my skis . . . and my haggis bag, and my skates and the woolly cap my Auntie Megsie knitted?'

He threw things out of drawers and hunted in cupboards.

'*Scotland the Brave*,' he sang . . .

The winter holiday was decided.

It is arranged

Dougal's room was crowded. Everyone was there, sitting wherever there was room. Florence, Brian, Mr MacHenry, Mr Rusty, Dylan and, half in and half out because of space problems, Ermintrude.

'Now are we all here?' said Dougal. He was wearing a tartan tammy and looked quite imposing. 'Is everyone *assembled*?'

'More or less, dear thing,' said Ermintrude. 'And we're all *agog*, aren't we?'

Everyone agreed that they were about as agog as they could get.

'I'm so agog I'm *hot*,' said Brian.

'Try getting off the stove,' said Dougal.

'Eek!' said Brian, getting off.

'Try not to interrupt too much, Brian,' murmured Florence.

Dougal took up an important position, adjusted his tammy and told them his plan.

They were to go to Scotland. Everyone would be accommodated with Dougal's Uncle Hamish, who had a large house. Dougal had sent a telegram to tell him they were coming, and everyone would assemble to leave, ready packed, in an hour's time.

Everyone started to talk at once. How could they go to Scotland? How would they know what to wear? How could they be ready in an hour's time?

'Silence!' shouted Dougal.

There was silence.

'I don't know what all the fuss is about,' he said. '*I'm* ready to leave.'

'But you *knew*!' they shrieked.

'All right! All right!' said Dougal. 'Just get ready as quickly as you can and we'll start.'

'Right!' said Florence. 'Everyone get ready.'

'EVERYONE GET READY!' shouted Brian. 'AND WE'LL START!'

They all went to get ready.

'Don't be long!' shouted Dougal.

'We won't,' they shouted back.

And they weren't. Much sooner than Dougal had expected they were all back, loaded with luggage and expectation.

Mr MacHenry was wearing an overcoat and a muffler, and carrying a canvas bag marked 'Epton MacHenry – Botanist'.

Mr Rusty also had an overcoat and a muffler and was dragging a large trunk labelled 'S.S. Titanic – THIS SIDE UP'.

Ermintrude had on a new hat covered in plastic daisies and was carrying a net full of hay with a large label on it saying 'HAY'.

Dylan was carrying a guitar, a rucksack and a large bunch of carrots.

Florence had a brand new ribbon in her hair and was carrying a school satchel marked 'FLORENCE – TOP IN GEOG' in red ink. She also had a very large basket labelled 'LUNCHEON'.

Brian had a blue case marked 'SAVOY HOTEL – LAUNDRY' and a large bag of lettuces.

He dumped these on Dougal's doorstep.

'How do we get there then?' he said.

Dougal paled.

'What?' he said, faintly.

'Oh, sorry,' said Brian, brightly, 'have I asked an awkward question?'

'Of course you haven't, Brian,' said Florence.

She turned to Dougal. His tammy had slipped right over his eyes and he seemed to be having difficulty breathing.

'Well?' she said.

Dougal opened his mouth to speak, but no sound came out except a high-pitched squeak.

'Are you all right, Dougal?' asked Florence, but before he could reply there was

a loud whistle and a train arrived outside
with a clank and a whoosh.

'You weren't thinking of leaving without
me, were you?' she hissed.

'NO!!' said Dougal, so loudly they all
jumped. 'No!! No!! Of course not! You're
taking us all to Scotland on holiday,
remember?'

'Scotland? Holiday?' said the train. 'I
never . . .'

But before she could say another word,
Dougal started to bundle everyone in.

'Come along! Come along! Don't dawdle!
We'll never get there!' he shouted.

The train gave a very loud whistle.
Everyone stopped.

'Now just a little moment,' said the train.
'If I'm taking you all to Scotland, one or two
requirements have to be met. There are
certain *rules* for journeys and I don't move a
single puff without them. First I shall need a
guard . . .'

'Me!' said Mr Rusty. 'I've always
wanted to be a guard – man and boy.'

'Good! OFF WE GO!' shouted Dougal.

The train whistled again.

'Not so fast,' she said. 'I need a ticket
collector and a buffet attendant and a stoker

and a chum to talk to during the dreary bits.'

Dougal groaned quietly.

'Be quicker by bicycle at this rate,' he muttered.

Dylan was chosen ticket collector.

Brian was elected stoker.

Mr MacHenry volunteered to ride up front and talk to the train when necessary.

All that was needed then was a cook and buffet attendant.

Everyone looked at Florence.

'Why are you all looking at me?' she said.

'You're a lady,' they said, 'and so a born provider.'

Florence sighed.

'Oh, all right,' she said. 'But don't expect too much.'

They all prepared to get on board, but Dougal made them wait while he went along the train painting big numbers on each carriage.

> 1   2   3   4

'What *are* you doing, Dougal?' they asked.

Dougal got in the carriage marked 1.

'You don't expect me to travel Second Class, do you?' he said.

'What about us?' they said.

'It's very simple,' said Dougal. 'As leader

and thinker I travel First Class. Miss Florence as cook and lady travels Second. Rabbits traditionally go Third, Mr MacHenry travels in the front and Mr Rusty in the guard's van.'

'What about pretty brown-eyed me?' said Brian.

'For you,' said Dougal, 'a special class has been created. It has never been used before – not even on the mail train to Siberia – FOURTH!'

'You're too good to me,' said Brian.

'Oh, get in,' said Dougal, 'and don't put your feet on the seat.'

'I haven't got any feet,' said Brian.

'Stop arguing!' shouted Dougal. 'All aboard! Here we go! Scots wha' hae!'

'Er . . . excuse me,' said Ermintrude, 'but I appear to have been overlooked.'

The train gave a toot and started to move.

'You're going without me!' wailed Ermintrude.

Everyone except Dougal leaned out of the windows and urged Ermintrude to get in before it was too late.

'But *where* shall I get in?' she puffed, running alongside.

'Anywhere!' they said.

So Ermintrude opened a door and got in.

'WHAT!! WHAT!! WHAT!!' screeched
Dougal. 'COWS DO NOT TRAVEL
FIRST!!'

'Too late!' they cried. 'We're moving.'

Dougal put his head out of the window.

'STOP!' he cried.

'TOO LATE!' they shouted.

'TOOT! TOOT!' went the train.

Dougal sighed, and sat down.

'How long is the journey, dear thing?' said
Ermintrude.

'I don't know,'
sighed Dougal, 'but it's
going to seem long.'

'St George for England;
St Pancras for Scotland!'
sang the train.

The journey

They left the garden and started the journey to Scotland. It was a good moment, like so many starts. Brian, stoking like anything, sang a song which sounded like: *Good thing Wendy's mouse looks stout,* but probably wasn't.

Florence was preparing lunch. She was a bit worried because she didn't have enough fish fingers for seven, but, as she said to herself, they could make up with a lot of mashed potato.

Mr MacHenry was listening to Brian singing and asking the train every now and again if she was all right.

The train *was* all right and enjoying the scenery around Watford.

Mr Rusty was busy guarding, looking out at every station and hoping they might stop so that he could do a bit of flag-waving.

Dylan had decided that as no one was paying there was no need to collect tickets, so he was sleeping instead.

Ermintrude was singing selections from Carmen.

Dougal was looking out of the window.

'What have I done to deserve it?' he
thought.

But by and large it was a happy trainful
and it seemed as though the journey to
Scotland would be completed in record time.

At Crewe, while the train filled herself with
what she assured everyone was water,
Florence served a light luncheon. Afterwards,
she made tea and lemonade and they all sat
in the buffet car talking about the journey.

'I should like to make absolutely certain of
the route,' said Mr Rusty, 'so that I know if
we go wrong or not.'

'How can we go wrong?' said Florence.

'We just keep going on up, don't we?'

'Can't be too careful,' said Mr Rusty.
'Now, what are the main stops?'

Dougal consulted a little map on the wall.

'It's quite simple,' he said. 'It's CREWE
(we've been there), CARLISLE,
GLASGOW, AUCHENSHUGGLE,
TILLIETUDLEM, GLENCOE and GLEN
DOUGAL.'

'BRISTOL! BRISTOL!' shouted a voice
outside. 'BRISTOL!'

'Bristol?!' said Dougal, faintly.

'Bristol?' said Mr MacHenry.

'I warned you,' said Mr Rusty.

Dougal rushed to the window and looked out. A porter was walking along the platform.

'Er . . . excuse me,' said Dougal. 'Is this Bristol?'

'Oh, no, me dear,' said the porter. 'It's Bognor Regis. I'm just shoutin' Bristol 'cos I likes the name.'

'Well, there's no need for sarcasm,' said Dougal, tartly.

'An' there's no need for soppy questions either,' said the porter, going away.

Dougal pulled his head back in.

'Now there's no need to panic,' he said. 'We musn't panic.'

'We have no intention of panicking, dear thing,' said Ermintrude. 'Why should we?'

'Er . . . I'll go and see what's happening,' said Mr Rusty. 'It's my duty.' And he went.

'I expect there's a perfectly simple explanation,' said Florence.

There was. Mr Rusty came back and explained that the train had taken a little detour to see a friend of hers who was about to retire from the railway service.

'We'll be going again soon,' he said.

'I don't know,' said Dougal, irritably. 'What a way to run a railway!'

'Don't worry,' said Florence.

'Don't worry?! Don't worry?!' said Dougal. 'Someone's got to worry. It would be a fine thing if nobody worried, wouldn't it?'

'Well, worrying won't start the train,' said Florence.

There was a jerk and the train started. Dougal looked at Florence.

'When's tea?' he said.

'I'll make it now,' sighed Florence.

The train went on while they all had tea. They discussed how long it might take to get to Scotland now that they'd detoured to Bristol. Dougal and Mr Rusty were a bit pessimistic but, as Florence said, the train was going very fast and they weren't likely to go out of their way again.

'I wish I could believe that,' said Dougal, gloomily. 'She's probably got a friend with 'flu at Aberystwyth.'

There was a jerk and a crash. The teacups scattered in all directions. Dougal fell on top of Brian. Dylan woke up and everyone else rolled about in all directions.

'What on earth's happening?' said Florence.

The train jerked and rolled and bumped.

'What's happening!?' shrieked Dougal.

They bumped and bumped and finally stopped.

'Listen!' said Mr MacHenry.

There was a noise, muffled and distant, but loud enough for everyone to hear.

Herroooff! it sounded like.

'We must have hit something,' said Florence.

Herroooff!! went the noise again.

'I shall go and investigate again,' said Mr Rusty. 'It's my duty.'

'I think we should all go,' said Florence, firmly. She didn't like the sound of that 'Herroooff!'

Herroooff!

The noise happened again, and this time it seemed a bit nearer.

'Listen,' whispered Dougal.

They all listened.

Herroooff!

'I think it's in here,' said Florence, faintly.

Herroooff!!

'It's near you, Dougal,' said Florence.

'What!' screeched Dougal, leaping up.

There was Brian, looking a bit squashed and a lot annoyed.

'Thank you,' he said. 'Too kind. Didn't you hear me shouting, you great woolly thing?'

'Steady, Brian,' said Florence.

'I'll never be steady again,' said Brian. 'I'm a squashed snail.'

'Do you good,' said Dougal, heartlessly.

'Oh, get off!' said Brian, and he went and sat down in a corner, looking like a snail who had been sat on by a dog.

The others, led by Dougal, went to see the train. They were in the middle of a field, and the train looked very disconsolate.

'I went off the rails,' she said, faintly. 'Is everyone all right?'

They assured her they were and helped her back on, Dougal leading the way and the others pushing and grunting. When she was back, Florence went to see her.

'All right now?' she asked. 'Pointing the right way?'

'Quite the right way, I think,' said the train, and she gave a little toot.

'All aboard,' said Mr Rusty, waving his

flag. Everyone got aboard and they started again.

'We'll take days at this rate,' said Dougal.

'I'm squashed,' moaned Brian.

'Then you won't want any cake, will you?' said Florence, briskly.

'I might force down a small piece,' said Brian.

So they all had some more tea and cake while the train went on.

They passed Carlisle safely. Then Glasgow.

'The Eternal City,' breathed Dougal, looking out.

Then Auchenshuggle.

Then Tillietudlem . . .

Dougal began to get excited.

'Glencoe!' he said. 'Oh, the beauty of it.'

He opened the window.

'Curse ye, Black Campbells!' he shrieked.

'Dougal, please!' said Florence.

'Sorry,' said Dougal. 'I was overcome.'

The train slowed. She gave a little toot. Dougal rushed to the window again.

'We've arrived!' he shouted. 'We've arrived! Oh, I'm so happy!'

'I'm squashed,' said Brian.

'Oh, be quiet!' they all shouted, rushing to the windows and looking out.

The train was pulling into a small station.
All around was snow and the big hills were
covered in pine trees all with snow on them
like thousands of Christmas trees.

'It's beautiful,' breathed Florence.

'Home!' said Dougal.

'Squashed,' said Brian.

The train stopped with a hiss. Everything
was quiet. Then from the far end of the
platform came a sound . . . a musical sound.

'The pipes!' whispered Dougal. 'Oh, the
pipes! I may cry!'

They all got out and stood on the platform.
Coming towards them, wearing a kilt and a
large plaid bonnet and playing a set of
bagpipes, was a small, black figure.

'Uncle Hamish,' breathed Dougal.

Scotland

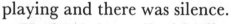

Uncle Hamish
advanced on them
playing the pipes
louder and louder
until finally, just as
he arrived, he stopped
playing and there was silence.

He fixed them all with glittering eyes.

'Where's wee Dougie?' he said, very loudly.

Everyone jumped and Mr Rusty laughed
nervously.

'Wee Dougie's here,' said Brian, pushing
Dougal forward with his nose.

Uncle Hamish looked at Dougal.

'Ye're late!' he said. 'Ye'll get no tea. And
put your tammy straight – ye look like Harry
Lauder's mother. Come!'

And he put the bag of his bagpipes under
his arm, blew powerfully, went quite red in
the face and stumped away down the
platform, the pipes wailing.

Dougal looked at the others.

'He's all right really,' he said, laughing nervously. 'It's just his way.'

'Lead on, wee Dougie,' said Brian.

'Any trouble out of you and I'll feed you to a Highland cow,' said Dougal.

'Oh, any about?' mooed Ermintrude.

'I think we'd better go before Uncle Hamish gets cross,' said Florence, and they all followed Dougal down the platform.

Uncle Hamish was waiting beside a huge, black open car covered with stickers saying 'Prevent Forest Fires'.

'Get in, get in,' he said, and they all got in.

'Ye'd better sit beside me, lassie,' he said to Florence.

Florence sat in the front seat while Uncle Hamish covered her right up to the chin with a tartan rug.

'Everyone ready?' he asked.

They were.

Uncle Hamish started the engine, put the car into gear, looked round at Florence, gave a huge wink and they were off.

Florence sat back.

'It's going to be all right,' she thought.

They drove away from the station and down a little lane on to the main road. It was

getting dark and a light snow began to fall.

'Is it far?' asked Florence.

'Just a step,' said Uncle Hamish. 'Sixty miles.' And he gave Florence another huge wink.

'Sixty miles!' said Mr Rusty.

'Just a step?' said Mr MacHenry.

'We'll be frozen solid!' said Dougal.

'If ye'd rather walk, ye can!' said Uncle Hamish, turning round and glittering at Dougal.

'Uncle . . . please, *please* look where you're going,' said Dougal, nervously.

Uncle Hamish turned back and stared down the road.

'No one would be foolish enough to get in *my* way,' he said.

'Not even trees?' said Brian, brightly, but Uncle Hamish was turning left through some huge iron gates.

'We're there,' he said.

'Sixty miles already?' said Ermintrude.

'My little joke,' boomed Uncle Hamish. 'Ha! Ha!'

He turned and looked at them.

'Ha! Ha!' they said, nervously.

The car pulled up in front of a huge, grey turreted house and they all got out clutching their luggage.

'Angus!' shouted Uncle Hamish, in a voice that would have penetrated lead. 'Where are ye, ye lop-sided lump of rubbish?!'

The great front door creaked open and out of it came a huge Highland bull. His horns measured a good six feet across and his eyes were completely covered in a mat of light brown hair.

'Ah, hush yer whisht!' he said.

'Dinna hush yer whisht to me!' shouted Uncle Hamish.

'And dinna shout at me, ye wee black

bannock!' bellowed Angus.

'Get my friends inside!' screeched Uncle
Hamish.

'Why, are they all helpless?' boomed Angus.

'I think we'd better go in,' whispered
Florence, and she went up the front steps
followed by the others.

Ermintrude was last. She passed Angus.

'Halloo,' she said.

Angus stopped glowering at Uncle Hamish
and looked at Ermintrude.

'Eh . . . let me carry yon hay for ye,
m'dear,' he said.

'Too kind,' murmured Ermintrude.

They all stood in the great hall. A huge fire was burning huge logs in the huge fireplace.

'Ye'll find your rooms marked clearly,' said Uncle Hamish.

'But first I expect ye'd like a little something?'

'Well, it has been a long day,' said Florence.

'Ye poor wee creatures,' said Uncle Hamish.

'ANGUS!! OPEN THE DOOR!!'

Angus walked slowly down the hall and pushed open a door. There, in a huge dining room with another huge fire burning more huge logs was a huge table laid with a huge meal. There were scones and potatoes and pies and cakes and carrots and lettuce and ice-cream and big pots of tea.

'Better get to it,' said Uncle Hamish, 'before it gets spoiled.'

So they all sat down to one of the best meals they'd ever had in their lives and afterwards they were very ready for bed.

Next morning Florence woke up very early. The frost had made patterns on her window and from outside came the sound of bagpipes. She went across to the window, rubbed a

little hole to see through, and looked out.
There was Uncle Hamish walking up and
down in the snow playing his pipes.

'Goodness, he must be cold,' thought
Florence.

There was a great booming clanging noise
outside the door. She peeped out. Angus was
walking slowly along the corridor banging a
gong strung between his horns. All down the
corridor doors opened and heads peered out.

'Breakfast!' bellowed Angus, banging his
way down the stairs.

And they all went down to breakfast.

Uncle Hamish came in and sat down at the head of the table.

'After ye've eaten,' he said, 'I want ye all changed into civilised apparel. And that means the kilt. Which tartan d'ye wear?'

He looked at them fiercely.

'Er . . . is there a MacCow?' said Ermintrude, nervously.

Uncle Hamish took a deep breath.

'Nay, there is not,' he said. 'Ye'll wear the Angus. What about you?' he said to Brian.

Brian choked on a cornflake.

'MacDougal,' he squeaked. 'What else?'

'Ye'll go far,' said Uncle Hamish.

He looked around.

'MacHenry,' said Mr MacHenry.

'There's no such clan,' said Uncle Hamish. He thought. 'Ye're never Irish, are ye?'

'It is possible,' said Mr MacHenry.

Uncle Hamish sighed.

'I can see it's little use,' he said. 'Ye'll all have to wear the true tartan. I've got a few in the great cupboard. Put them on.'

He drank a cup of tea, ate seven kippers in quick succession and stumped out.

'He's a character,' said Mr Rusty.

'He is that,' said Mr MacHenry, and after

breakfast they all dressed themselves in the
true tartan. Brian had a little difficulty
because of his lack of waist and legs, but they
finally all assembled in the great hall and
waited for anything that might happen.

Uncle Hamish came in. Behind him was
Angus with a bag and a hamper.

'All set then?' said Uncle Hamish.

'Er . . . for what, Uncle Hamish?' said
Dougal.

'Well, 'tis Tuesday,' said Uncle Hamish.
'And on Tuesdays, rain or shine, snow or
sleet, sun or typhoon, we hunt the haggis.'

'Er . . . will we be back for lunch?' said Dougal.

Uncle Hamish glittered.

'Can ye think of nothing but your tum, laddie?' he roared. 'Come, we're away.'

'How exciting,' breathed Florence.

Mr MacHenry asked if it would be all right for him to be excused the haggis hunt; he would prefer to look around the gardens. Mr Rusty said that would suit him better too.

'Please yourselves,' said Uncle Hamish. 'Come, we're away.'

'Follow me, me dear,' whispered Angus to Ermintrude. 'I've got the picnic basket.'

'What are ye whispering about, ye great lummock?' roared Uncle Hamish.

'Ah, hist!' said Angus. 'Can I not whisper now?'

Uncle Hamish glowered.

'Come, we're away,' he said.

'How exciting,' breathed Florence.

And they set off on the haggis hunt.

Haggis hunt

Outside, Uncle Hamish stood by a large
open cart. Harnessed to the cart was a horse
smoking a long cigar. He had one front leg
crossed over the other and looked a bit bored.

'Come away, all,' shouted Uncle Hamish,
and they all got into the cart.

'Up! Up! Big John,' said Uncle Hamish.
The horse uncrossed his legs and began to pull
the cart very slowly down the drive towards
the big iron gates.

'Big John!' shouted Uncle Hamish, 'I'll
trouble ye to break into a trot.'

The horse looked over his shoulder.

'That'll be the day,' he drawled, going slowly on. Uncle Hamish glowered but said nothing.

'Why's he called Big John?' whispered Florence.

'Ah, now,' said Uncle Hamish, loudly. 'He was once in a Cowboy and Indian film and he's never been the same since.'

'Get away,' said Big John.

The cart moved slowly along the road through the snow; Florence in the front with Uncle Hamish; Brian, Dougal and Dylan in the middle; and Angus and Ermintrude sitting on the picnic basket at the back, giggling a lot.

They turned off the road through a gate marked 'No Trespassers – No Campbells'.

'Why does it say "No Campbells", Uncle Hamish?' asked Florence.

'I'll not have a Campbell on my land,' said Uncle Hamish, sternly.

'Why?' said Florence.

'Because they're black-hearted, fierce and untrustworthy,' said Uncle Hamish.

'Oh,' said Florence.

They went along a lane through dark pine woods. The lane went up and up, twisting and turning until it reached the end of the trees and there, by a big dead pine, they stopped.

'We start here,' said Uncle Hamish, unhitching Big John and giving him a nosebag. 'Out, everybody.'

Dylan had fallen asleep in the bottom of the cart, but everyone else got out.

'We'll go in two's,' said Uncle Hamish. 'Ye'll come with me, lassie,' he said to Florence.

'And ye'll come with me, lassie,' said Angus to Ermintrude.

Brian turned to Dougal.

'Don't say it!' said Dougal. 'My first haggis hunt,' he groaned, 'and I'm saddled with a snail.'

'What about Dylan?' said Florence.

'Yon rabbit can do as he pleases,' said

Uncle Hamish, and as Dylan seemed pleased to sleep, they left him.

'We'll go three ways and meet back here for lunch,' said Uncle Hamish. 'Take care the wee beasties don't outfox ye.' And he set off with Florence at a brisk trot.

Angus and Ermintrude went another way, not quite so briskly, and Brian looked at Dougal again.

'Have you even the remotest idea what to do?' he asked, brightly.

'No, I haven't,' said Dougal, crossly.

Big John looked over his nosebag.

'You need to creep up and surround them,' he drawled.

'How can I creep up and surround them?' said Dougal. 'I don't even know what they look like.'

'Oh,' said Big John, 'you can't miss them. They're round and fat and they go "whee!" a lot.'

'They sound lovely,' said Brian. 'Are there many about?'

'Something like two million at the last count,' said Big John.

'Not dangerous, I take it,' said Dougal, casually.

'Depends,' said Big John, laconically.

'On what?' said Dougal, nervously.

'On whether they're crept up on and surrounded,' said Big John, and he closed both eyes and sat down.

'Oh, well, better show willing, I suppose' said Brian. 'Come on.'

'I've gone off the whole idea, but Uncle Hamish will expect me to catch one, I suppose,' said Dougal, and he followed Brian through the snow and up the hill.

Brian was enjoying himself. He slid uphill and he slid downhill. Dougal plodded along behind, his sporran full of snow and the fringes of his kilt covered with icicles. His head was low and his eyes on the ground.

'Whee!' said Brian, going down a little hill.

'Take cover!' screeched Dougal, going head first into a drift.

Brian came back.

'What are you doing in there?' he asked.

'I heard one,' said Dougal. 'It went "whee!" '

'Oh, sorry, that was me,' said Brian.

Dougal pulled himself out of the snow and shook.

'And why, pray, were you going "whee!"?' he asked.

'I just felt like it ,' said Brian.

'Well, the next time you feel like it, let me know,' said Dougal.

'Carry me then,' said Brian.

'Certainly not,' said Dougal.

They went on. The snow got deeper and the hill got steeper.

Suddenly, 'whee! whee!' they heard.

'Was that you?' whispered Dougal.

'No,' whispered Brian.

'Whee! whee!' they heard again.

Dougal went whiter than the snow.

'It's a haggis,' he said, faintly.

'Whee! whee!'

'And it's coming this way,' said Brian.

'Whee! whee! WHEEEE! ! !'

A small, round tartan object hurtled over their heads and landed in a flurry of snow a few feet away.

It moved a little, and then was still.

Dougal and Brian moved towards it.

'Not very big,' whispered Brian.

'Whee!' it said suddenly, and Dougal and Brian somersaulted backwards into the soft snow.

The haggis looked at them with two piercing black eyes.

'Ye're not much good at it, are ye?' it said. 'Ye're supposed to creep up and surround me. I heard ye coming two miles awa'.'

'We've never done it before,' said Brian. 'Sir.'

'I can well tell yon,' said the haggis. 'Are ye with Hamish's lot?'

Dougal and Brian confessed that they were.

'Aye, yon Hamish,' said the haggis, wheezing with laughter. 'Fifty years after the haggis and he's never caught one yet.'

'Have we caught you?' said Brian.

'Ye have *not*,' said the haggis, 'but you're welcome to try. You have to creep up and surround me.'

'So we understand,' said Dougal.

'What happens if we do?' said Brian.

'Then I'm captured,' said the haggis.

'And if we don't?' said Dougal, nervously.

'Then ye have to go to Oban for a new haggis-hunting licence,' said the haggis. 'And Oban's a long way,' it wheezed. 'Are ye ready?'

They said they were.

'Away we go then,' said the haggis, and it shot straight up in the air with a 'whee' and disappeared like a bullet in the direction of Norway.

Dougal sat down.

'This is hopeless,' he said. 'It's about a hundred miles away by now and I'm *cold*.'

'We don't want to be thought failures though, do we?' said Brian.

'Why not?' said Dougal.

'That's not the attitude,' said Brian, sternly. 'Come on, old chum. Up! Up! Deep breaths!'

'Oh, stop being so outdoor and hearty,' said Dougal.

Brian climbed up a little hill and slid down again.

'I've got a marvellous idea,' he said. 'We'll *make* one.'

'We'll *what*?' said Dougal.

'Make a haggis,' said Brian, 'and pretend we crept up on it and surrounded it and captured it. Get your kilt off.'

'I will not!' said Dougal. 'The idea . . .'

'This is no time for arguing,' said Brian. 'Get it off!'

'Only under protest,' said Dougal with dignity, and he took his kilt off and gave it to Brian.

Brian spread it on the ground and pushed snow into it.

'Pat it so that it's round,' he said.

'You pat it,' said Dougal. 'I provided the kilt.'

'I can't pat without hands,' said Brian, with exasperation. 'I'm doing this for *you*, you know.'

'I'm truly grateful,' said Dougal, sarcastically. But he patted the snow into a round ball and fastened the kilt round it. It looked just like a haggis except for the eyes.

'What about the eyes?' he said.

'Paint!' said Brian.

'Brilliant!' said Dougal. 'It just so happens I have a gallon of paint in me sporran. Great clump!'

'Don't be like that,' said Brian, and he

burrowed into the snow until he had cleared a little patch.

'We'll use mud,' he said. 'Sit down there.'

'Why?' said Dougal.

'The ground's frozen – we'll have to warm it,' said Brian.

Dougal sat down.

'The things I do,' he said, heavily.

Meanwhile, back at the cart, the others had returned from the haggis hunt empty-handed. They sat down while Angus spread the picnic and soon they were all eating huge sandwiches and drinking bottles of milk.

'Didn't catch many, did we?' said Florence, brightly.

'Nay,' said Uncle Hamish, gloomily.

'Do you usually catch a lot?' said Florence.

'Nay,' said Uncle Hamish.

'What's the most you've ever caught?' said Florence.

'He's never caught one,' bellowed Angus. 'Never a one!'

'Silence, ye crummock!' shouted Uncle Hamish.

'Ha!' scoffed Angus. 'Never a one!'

'I wonder where Dougal and Brian have got to?' said Florence, trying to change the subject.

'Up to their sporrans in a drift, I shouldn't wonder,' said Uncle Hamish. 'Pass the sandwiches, lassie.'

There was a shout. Dougal and Brian appeared on the brow of the hill holding something up.

'I think they've caught one,' breathed Florence. 'How exciting.'

'Aye,' said Uncle Hamish, not appearing to be too pleased.

Dougal and Brian arrived breathless.

'Where's your kilt, Dougal?' said Florence.

'I lost it in the battle with this haggis,' said Dougal, quickly.

'Ye got one then?' said Uncle Hamish, slowly.

'Yes,' said Dougal.

'Aye,' said Brian.

Uncle Hamish inspected the haggis Brian and Dougal had brought.

'Aye,' he said. 'A good specimen. We'll hang it in the hall over the great fire. Aye.'

Dougal went pale and choked on a sandwich.

'Over the great fire?' said Brian.

'Aye,' said Uncle Hamish. ''Tis the first and it shall have the place of honour next to the salmon caught on the Tay in '89 by Queen Victoria.'

'Er . . . Uncle Hamish,' said Dougal. 'Shouldn't we just let it go perhaps?'

'Let it go!' shouted Uncle Hamish. 'My first haggis?'

'We caught it,' squeaked Brian.

'On *my* land,' said Uncle Hamish, sternly, 'and on the wall over the fire it shall go. Come, we'll be away back.'

They packed up the picnic and all got into the cart, Uncle Hamish putting the haggis under his seat.

'Now, Big John,' he said. 'Home – at a gallop.'

'That'll be the day,' said Big John, pulling the cart slowly away down the lane.

Dougal and Brian sat together nervously while the cart jolted along.

'Fine mess you've got me into,' muttered Dougal.

'I did my best,' muttered Brian.

'What's that . . . like . . . muttering?' said Dylan, waking up. 'Have I missed anything?'

'Oh, go back to sleep,' said Dougal.

'I will, man,' said Dylan, and he pulled the haggis out from under the seat, put his head on it and went to sleep again.

They jogged on.

Suddenly Brian nudged Dougal.

'Look!' he whispered.

'Oh, my,' said Dougal, looking.

A trickle of water was running along the bottom of the cart. It was the haggis, melting rapidly.

'He's melting it!' said Brian. 'Quick, get it out.'

Dougal pulled the haggis out from under Dylan's head. It unrolled completely and a ball of squashy snow tumbled slowly off the back of the cart.

'What shall we do?' moaned Dougal.

'Put the kilt on,' whispered Brian, urgently.

'It's all soggy,' hissed Dougal.

'Never mind that,' said Brian.

Dougal put his wet kilt back on and waited apprehensively as they jogged along.

When they got back it was getting dark. Uncle Hamish got down and reached under the seat. He fumbled and felt.

'It's gone!' he thundered.

'Gone?' said Florence.

'Gone?' said Dougal, in a high-pitched voice.

'I *thought* I heard a "whee!"' said Brian.

Uncle Hamish was silent for a moment and then he said in a voice which seemed quite pleased, 'Ah, well! They're cunning wee beasties. Come, we'll have some tea,'

'I see you got your kilt back, Dougal,' whispered Florence, significantly.

'Don't be rotten,' said Dougal, and they all went in to tea.

Toboganning

At breakfast next morning no mention was made of the haggis hunt. Instead, after his usual batch of kippers, Uncle Hamish suggested they might like to amuse themselves as he was going to be busy.

'I've work to do,' he said, 'but ye'll find plenty of diversion, I've no doubt.'

Florence assured him that they would and he wasn't to worry about them.

'Och, I'll not worry about ye,' said Uncle Hamish, stumping off. 'Enjoy yourselves.'

They sat round the table wondering what to do.

'If we had some skis, we could ski,' said Florence.

'If we had a toboggan, we could toboggan,' said Ermintrude.

'If we had some ice-skates, we could ice-skate,' said Mr MacHenry.

'And if we had any sense we could think of something,' said Brian.

'All right, clever breeks,' said Dougal, '*you* think of something.'

'I have,' said Brian.

They waited. Brian buttered a piece of toast.

'Well, tell us then!' said Dougal, furiously.

'Plead with me,' said Brian.

'Really, you are *impossible*,' said Dougal. 'And you've got butter all over your nose.'

'Perhaps if you *could* tell us Brian . . .?' said Florence.

Brian rubbed his nose on the tablecloth to wipe the butter off.

'Has it gone?' he asked.

They assured him it had and waited, expectantly.

'Tin trays,' said Brian.

'Tin trays?!' said Dougal.

'Tin trays,' said Brian. 'They make good toboggans . . . I remember.'

'Brian, you are clever,' said Florence.

'Huh! *Anyone* could have thought of *that*,' said Dougal.

'Then why didn't you?' said Florence.

'My mind was on higher things,' said Dougal, loftily, 'but I would have got round to it.'

'There's only one little problem as I see it, dear things,' said Ermintrude, 'and that is where to acquire these tin trays.'

'A house like this is sure to have tin trays,' said Mr Rusty. 'Houses like this always do.'

'Then we'll go on a search,' said Florence, 'and meet in the hall in ten minutes.'

'You're a born organiser, dear heart,' said Ermintrude. And they all left to look for tin trays.

Ten minutes later, in the hall, they were all assembled again.

Brian had a tin tray. It was marked 'Primrose Tea Rooms. Scones Four a Penny'.

Dougal also had a tray. It was long and thin and covered with a picture of Skelmorlie in the autumn.

Florence had found a large biscuit tin just big enough to sit in and Dylan had the lid, also just big enough to sit in.

Mr Rusty and Mr MacHenry were very pleased with themselves because they had found four flat pieces of wood and were busy working out ways of attaching them to their feet with string.

Ermintrude had failed. She came in with a tin lid about ten centimetres across.

'I don't think it will hold me,' she said, sadly.

'I don't think a barn door would hold *you*,' giggled Dougal.

'Cheeky thing,' said Ermintrude. 'Just for that I shall ride with you.'

Dougal paled.

'We'll take turns,' he said, quickly.

So they all wrapped up warm and went out.

Outside, Big John was leaning nonchalantly against the wall.

'Hello, Big John,' said Florence.

'Hi!' said Big John. 'Going some place?'

'Tobogganing,' said Florence.

'Waal, that's nice,' said Big John. 'I reckon Ben Bumpy would be the best place.'

'What's Ben Bumpy?' said Florence.

'A mountain,' said Big John.

'Is it far, dear horse?' said Ermintrude.

''Bout half a mile,' said Big John, '. . . as the crow flies.'

'And as the dog trudges?' said Dougal.

''Bout four miles,' said Big John. 'Straight up.'

'That's not so good,' said Mr Rusty. 'Especially at my age.'

''Course, if I'd a mind I could take you,' said Big John.

'And have you a mind?' said Brian, brightly.

'Might,' said Big John.

'I wonder how long this fascinating conversation will go on?' whispered Dougal.

'Hush, Dougal,' said Florence. 'We'd be grateful for a lift, Big John.'

'Hitch up then,' said Big John, and as he moved away from the wall they saw he had attached to his harness a long rope.

'An animated ski-lift,' said Dougal. 'Now I've seen everything.'

They sat on their various trays, stood on their various skis, caught hold of the rope and Big John started off, pulling them along like a giant tail.

'I'm having to walk,' wailed Ermintrude.

'Get on somewhere,' they shouted.

'Where?' said Ermintrude.

'Anywhere!' they said.

So Ermintrude got on.

'Comfy, dear heart?' she said.

'The things I suffer,' said Dougal.

And Big John pulled them four miles straight up Ben Bumpy.

At the top it was beautiful. The sun was shining and glancing on the snow and they could see the sea glittering a long way off.

'Aren't we lucky?' said Florence.

'Lucky?' said Dougal. 'I've just travelled four miles with my bottom in the snow.'

They stood at the top and looked down.

'Er . . . who's going to be first?' said Mr Rusty.

It seemed a long way and no one was very keen to be first down.

Brian sat on his tray.

'I provided the notion,' he said, 'and I think someone else should provide the first run.'

'You're absolutely right, mollusc,' said Dougal, evilly, sidling up behind Brian. 'Oops! I've slipped! Oh, dear!' And he gave Brian a little push.

'Help!' said Brian. 'Helllllp . . .'

'Quite a good turn of speed,' said Dougal, giggling, 'for a snail.'

And he laughed so much he sat down heavily on his tray.

'Help!' he said. 'Helllllp . . .'

'I don't think he meant to do that,' said Ermintrude, watching Dougal disappear.

'Perhaps you'd all care for a snack while we wait for them?' said Mr MacHenry. 'I just happened to bring a little something with me.'

'How thoughtful,' murmured Florence.

Meanwhile, half-way down the slope, Dougal was catching up with Brian very rapidly. Brian was enjoying himself.

'Whee,' he shouted, 'Whee!!'

Dougal slid swiftly on.

'Get out of the way!' he screeched.

Brian looked round.

'Eek!' he squeaked. 'You're bearing down on me! I hate being beared down on!'

'I can't help it!' shouted Dougal. 'Get out of the way.'

'Steer round me!' shouted Brian.

'I can't!' screamed Dougal.

'But you're not trying!' shouted Brian.

Dougal got closer and closer. There was a sharp clang.

'Welcome aboard,' said Brian.

'Only half of me's aboard,' moaned Dougal.

'Well, you weren't fully invited,' said Brian.

Ahead of them a large mound of snow loomed up.

'We'll go over it!' shouted Brian, happily.

They didn't go over it; they went into it.

The others, watching from the top of the hill, saw Dougal and Brian hit the bank of snow and disappear.

'They've disappeared,' said Mr MacHenry.

'Do you think they're all right?' said Florence, anxiously.

'Of course, dear heart,' said Ermintrude. 'It's very soft snow.'

'Well, I think I'm going to see,' said Florence bravely, and she got in her biscuit tin.

'Er . . . goodbye,' she said.

'Give them our love,' they said.

'Er . . . no one else coming?' said Florence.

'We don't think so,' they said.

'Er . . . I'll be going then,' said Florence.

'Goodbye,' they said, giving her a little push.

Meanwhile, back in the snow, Dougal and Brian looked around. They were in an icy cavern and there was a dark tunnel leading out of it.

'That's a very dark tunnel,' said Brian.

'Nervous, snail?' said Dougal.

'Yes,' said Brian, 'aren't you?'

'Certainly not,' said Dougal.

There was a snuffling, grunting noise from the tunnel.

'I am now,' said Dougal.

A long black and white nose appeared out of the tunnel, followed by a black and white head and a black and white body.

It was a badger.

'Can I help you?' he said, mildly.

'Well, not really,' said Brian, 'we . . . er . . . just dropped in.'

'I see you have a tray with you,' said the badger, 'and whilst this is not actually a cafeteria I could provide a cup of tea if you so wish.'

He disappeared down the tunnel.

'We've got a right one here,' whispered Dougal, and he sat down very suddenly with a shriek as a biscuit tin hit him in the back.

'Hello,' said Florence. 'I was looking for you.'

'Just in time for tea,' said Brian.

Meanwhile, back on the hill, the others had watched Florence's progress with interest.

'The dear girl's disappeared too,' said Ermintrude. 'I think this now calls for a search party.'

'How many do you think constitutes a search party?' said Mr Rusty, nervously.

'Everyone,' said Ermintrude, firmly. 'Come along. Best feet forward.'

And she stepped on Mr Rusty's skis and slid rapidly down the hill.

'She's taken my skis, so I can't go,' said Mr Rusty.

'Borrow mine,' said Mr MacHenry.

'No, thank you,' said Mr Rusty.

But Dylan thought they should all go.

'Safety in numbers, men,' he said.

So on two skis and a biscuit tin lid they set out bravely.

Meanwhile, back in the badger's hallway, Florence and Brian and Dougal were drinking tea and the badger was apologising because he had no biscuits.

'I didn't expect anyone, you see,' he said.

'Please don't worry,' said Florence.

'Well, no, I won't worry,' said the badger. 'But I expect you were using the phrase politely because I imagine you wouldn't necessarily think that lack of biscuits would really tax my peace of mind. . . .'

'He's off again,' whispered Dougal.

There was a flurry of snow and Ermintrude's head appeared.

'I'll just get another cup,' said the badger, and he went.

In quick succession Mr Rusty, Mr MacHenry and Dylan arrived in the icy hall.

'Bit crowded,' said Brian, taking the point of Mr Rusty's ski out of his ear.

The badger came back.

'Er . . . I hope we're not intruding?' said Mr Rusty.

'Intruding?' said the badger. 'Ah, now, well. Intrusion. To enter uninvited. To thrust oneself in forcibly and unwelcome. I suppose strictly speaking you have forced yourself in and you have entered uninvited, but as you are welcome I think we can safely say you are not intruding. I'll just get some more cups.'

'He must have a lot of cups,' said Brian.

They all had tea and the badger told them he lived alone and didn't see many strangers.

'I hope you will come again,' he said.

'Thank you,' said Florence. 'Er . . . I think we should go now.'

'Thank you for the tea,' they said.

'I'll just see you out,' said the badger.

Outside, Big John was waiting.

'Hello, Big John,' said the badger. 'Leg better?'

'Waal,' said Big John. 'It depends what you mean by better.'

'Let us say in the sense that it is not as bad as it was before,' said the badger.

'In that case, yes,' said Big John.

'Good,' said the badger.

'They do go on, don't they?' whispered Dougal.

'Just a tidge,' said Brian.

They all hitched up on Big John's rope and waved goodbye to the badger.

'Go safely,' he said.

'Goodbye, Mr Campbell,' said Big John.

And they all went home.

MISC.
BALLS

Golf

One day, Brian and Dougal were having a look round in Uncle Hamish's loft. It was full of things and very dusty. There were dozens of old trunks and hatboxes, old broken chairs and cracked jugs, bundles of newspapers and boxes with string round them.

'What a great place,' said Brian, his head in a box.

Dougal sneezed.

'Oh, come out,' he said.

Brian came out and pounced on something lying in a corner.

'Hey, look!' he said. 'What's *this*?'

Dougal looked. It was a long bag and as Brian pulled it out, it rattled.

'That's a golf bag,' said Dougal, thoughtfully.

The bag had lots of little labels hanging from the handle. They read them.

'Hamish MacDougal. TROON 1923.'

'Hamish MacDougal. CARNOUSTIE 1931.'

'Hamish MacDougal. OPEN CHAMPION ST ANDREWS.'

'Open Champion!' breathed Dougal. 'Uncle Hamish! Well!'

'What's an Open Champion?' said Brian.

'It just means that Uncle Hamish was the best golfer in the world, that's all,' said Dougal. 'I wonder why he never told us?'

'Probably because we never asked him,' said Brian. 'Hey, why don't we have a game? Perhaps I could be Open Champion.'

'You couldn't be Open Champion if you were the only one playing,' said Dougal, scathingly.

'Let's play, anyway,' said Brian, 'it looks like a fun game.'

'It's not supposed to be *fun*,' said Dougal. 'It's *golf* and it's very *serious*.'

Uncle Hamish was in the hall when they went down with the golf clubs.

'Why didn't you tell us you were Open Champion?' said Dougal.

'I wasn't asked,' said Uncle Hamish.

'Will you have a game?' squeaked Brian.

Uncle Hamish looked the golf clubs over.

'Aye, it's been a long time,' he said,
slowly. 'A long time since I played. ANGUS!!'

Angus appeared.

'Put out my plus-fours and my spikey shoes,'
said Uncle Hamish, 'we're off to the links.'

Angus roared with laughter.

'At your age?'
he bellowed.
'Ye'll not see the
ball, let alone hit it!'

'Will ye do as ye're told?' screamed Uncle
Hamish. 'My plus-fours and my spikey shoes,
if you please!!'

'I gave your plus-fours to the Women's
Rural Jumble Sale twenty years ago,' said
Angus, 'and your spikey shoes to Oxfam.'

'Ye'd no right!' screeched Uncle Hamish.

'Wear your brogues if ye're set on yon
foolishness,' said Angus, picking up the
clubs.

So Uncle Hamish put on his brogues and they set out for the golf course.

'I've never played golf,' said Brian, chattily.

'Then ye've never lived,' said Uncle Hamish.

They arrived at the course.

'Go into that shop,' said Uncle Hamish, 'say I sent you and ask Willie MacNuckle for some clubs to use.'

Dougal and Brian did so.

'This is a *shop*?' whispered Brian.

It was full of golf clubs and golf bags and golf balls and golf hats and golf woollies and golf umbrellas.

'It's a *golf* shop,' whispered Dougal.

'I'd never have guessed,' giggled Brian.

'Nae giggling in my shop,' said a voice, sternly.

'Er . . . Mr MacNuckle?' said Dougal.

'Aye,' said Mr MacNuckle.

He was a little man with a huge red beard.

'Er . . . we want to borrow some clubs,' said Dougal. 'Uncle Hamish said you'd lend us some.'

'Do ye want a set each, or will one be enough?' he asked.

'Oh, I think one will be plenty,' said Brian. 'I'm not playing.'

'I'm relieved to hear that,' murmured
Dougal.

Willie produced a set of clubs. Dougal
picked them up, and nearly fell over.

'They're a bit heavy,' he said.

Willie sighed.

'Would ye like a trolley?' he said.

'We'd love a trolley,' said Brian.

So Willie put the clubs on a little trolley
and Dougal and Brian joined Uncle Hamish
on the first tee, which was a little patch of
grass.

Uncle Hamish walked on to it.

'Driver,' he said to Angus.

'Driver?' whispered Brian. 'Where's he going?'

'It's a golf club,' hissed Dougal.

Uncle Hamish put a ball on a little peg, gave a swish or two with his club and then hit the ball with a great crack. It shot away into the distance and Uncle Hamish strode away after it, followed by Angus who was muttering to himself.

'I think they've forgotten us,' said Brian, but they followed on with their bag and their trolley.

When they caught up, Uncle Hamish and

Angus were looking at a little flag set on a
stick about 175 yards away.

'Spoon,' said Uncle Hamish.

'Spoon?' said Angus. 'Are ye mad? Take
the cleek.'

'Will ye give me the spoon and stop
blethering!' screamed Uncle Hamish.

Angus silently gave Uncle Hamish a club
and Uncle Hamish, after another swish or
two, hit the ball another great crack. It
soared up into the air and then came down,
down, down and finally landed right beside
the little flag.

Uncle Hamish gave the club back to
Angus. Angus put the club in the bag.

'Ye'd have done better with yer cleek,' he
said, and they both strode away.

'Good game, isn't it?' said Brian, brightly.

'Oh, come on!' said Dougal.

They caught up again. Angus was holding
the flag and Uncle Hamish was looking
intently at his ball which was lying very close
to a little hole.

'Er . . . Uncle Hamish . . .' said Dougal.

'Whisht!' said Uncle Hamish. 'I've a birdie
here.'

'A birdie?' hissed Brian. 'Where?'

'How should I know?' said Dougal.

'Perhaps it's down the hole.'

Uncle Hamish walked round and looked at the ball from the other side.

'Och, get on with it,' muttered Angus. ''Tis dead.'

'A dead birdie?' whispered Brian. 'How sad.'

'I think it's golfing talk,' hissed Dougal.

Uncle Hamish finally made up his mind, took a club from the bag and, with a great indrawing of breath, tapped the ball into the hole.

'Lucky,' muttered Angus.

They walked off to another patch of grass.

'Er . . . Uncle Hamish,' said Dougal, but Uncle Hamish was busy studying another little flag – this time a much nearer one.

'Niblick,' he said to Angus.

'Niblick?' said Angus. 'At your age? 'Tis a mashie-niblick at least.'

'Niblick!' roared Uncle Hamish.

'Ye're mad!' bellowed Angus.

'Will ye give me my niblick and stop chuntering?' said Uncle Hamish.

Angus silently gave Uncle Hamish a club.

'I find this quite fascinating,' whispered Brian.

Uncle Hamish swished the club again, gave a look towards the flag and hit the ball another great click. It sped up very high and came down again, bouncing on the green, this time hitting the flag-stick and stopping dead a short distance from the little hole.

Uncle Hamish handed the club back to Angus.

'Ye'd have done better wi' yer mashie-niblick,' said Angus.

'Ah, away with ye,' said Uncle Hamish, striding off.

'Do you think we should go home?' said Brian.

But Dougal was determined.

'Give me a club,' he said.

'You're never going to hit a ball,' said Brian, aghast.

'Yes, I am,' said Dougal. 'Give me a club.'

'Do you want a spoon, a cleek, a mashie or a baffy?' said Brian.

'Do you know which is which?' said Dougal, coldly.

'I could have a guess,' said Brian, happily.

'Oh, just give me one,' said Dougal.

Brian rummaged.

'There's a nice wooden one here,' he said.

'That'll do,' said Dougal, taking the club and walking on to the tee.

'I hope you know what you're doing,' said Brian, anxiously.

'Oh, be quiet,' said Dougal.

He set his ball on a little peg just as Uncle Hamish had done and took a swish or two.

'Watch where it goes!' he screamed, and aimed a great blow at the ball.

There was silence.

'Did you watch it?' asked Dougal.

'Yes,' said Brian.

'Then where did it go?' demanded Dougal.

'It's still there,' said Brian.

Dougal looked down.

'Well, watch it this time,' he muttered,
'and stop messing about.'

'Sorry,' said Brian.

Dougal took another swish or two, looked
hard at the ball and aimed another mighty
blow at it.

The ball shot straight up into the air.

'Did you see it?' shouted Dougal.

'It's gone up,' said Brian.

They looked. The ball was still rising. As
they watched, it started to descend towards
the flag where Uncle Hamish and Angus
were looking at their ball.

'Oh, dear,' said Brian.

The ball came down, down, down, landed on the green, hit Uncle Hamish's ball and dropped into the hole.

'You've done it now,' said Brian, happily.

They walked slowly up to the green where Uncle Hamish and Angus were waiting.

'Er . . . sorry,' said Dougal.

'Ye should be,' said Uncle Hamish. 'But it was a bonny shot all the same. Did ye use the niblick?'

'Er . . . something like that,' said Dougal, nervously.

'Huh!' said Angus, loudly.

'Huh!' said Brian, quietly.

'Well, we'll see how ye fare on the next,' said Uncle Hamish. 'Come away.'

He went to the next patch.

On the tee Uncle Hamish was warming up, swinging a club.

'A long hole, this,' he said. 'My favourite.'

'Er . . . where *is* the hole?' said Dougal.

Uncle Hamish pointed. Away in the distance, just visible, fluttered a little flag.

'525 yards,' said Angus.

'Is there a bus?' said Brian.

'Shall I show the way?' said Uncle Hamish to Dougal.

'Please do,' said Dougal.

'Driver,' said Uncle Hamish, and Angus gave him a club. He hit the ball. It went a long way straight towards the flag.

'That'll do,' he said.

Dougal stepped up to the tee.

'Driver,' he said, and Brian handed him a club.

'Is that right?' he hissed.

'How should I know?' hissed Dougal back.

He sat the ball on its peg, closed his eyes and hit. There was a sharp crack and the ball sped away towards the flag.

'That'll do,' said Dougal, nonchalantly.

They set off towards where the two balls were lying. Dougal's had gone a little way beyond Uncle Hamish's.

Uncle Hamish hit his ball a great thwack and again it went straight and true towards the flag.

'Your turn,' he said to Dougal.

Dougal turned to Brian.

'Spoon,' he said.

'Spoon?!' said Brian. 'That's never a spoon shot. Take your mashie-tattie . . .'

And he giggled like anything.

'Have you gone quite off your head?' said Dougal. 'GIE ME YON SPOON!!'

Uncle Hamish nodded approvingly, and

Brian handed Dougal a club.

Dougal stood over the ball, hoping his luck would hold.

He aimed and swung.

The ball stayed where it was, but the club went sideways like a bullet, hit a tree with a sharp crack, bounced straight up in the air, came down again, hit a stone, shot back towards Dougal and landed at his feet.

He laughed nervously.

'Just practising,' he said.

'Oh, aye?' said Uncle Hamish.

Dougal hit the ball quickly. It went along the ground like a rabbit and ended up just beside Uncle Hamish's.

'Oh, aye,' said Uncle Hamish.

'We'll be late for tea if we're not careful,' said Angus.

'We'll finish this hole,' said Uncle Hamish, and he strode away.

'A word of warning,' said Angus.

'Yes?' said Dougal.

'Don't beat him,' said Angus, 'or there'll be trouble.'

'What sort of trouble?' said Brian.

'Terrible trouble,' said Angus.

Uncle Hamish was looking at his ball.

'That's two shots to me and two shots to

you,' he said to Dougal.

'Does that mean we're winning?' said Brian.

'It does not,' said Uncle Hamish.

He gave his ball a little hit and it rolled up very close to the hole and stopped.

He went over and tapped it in.

'Four,' he said. 'Ye need that to win.'

'I need what to win?' said Dougal.

'Ye need to put that ball in that hole in one more stroke and ye win,' said Uncle Hamish, and from the look on his face he didn't think it was very likely to happen.

Dougal took a club out of the bag without looking, went up to his ball and hit it.

It went sideways, hit Angus on a horn, bounced on Brian's shell, over Uncle Hamish's foot and into the hole.

'Oh, lawks!' whispered Brian.

'Come, Angus,' said Uncle Hamish,
slowly. 'We'll away.'

When they got back Florence was pouring
tea.

'Well, what have you two been doing?' she
asked, brightly.

'We've been cleeking the mashies with a
brassie baffy . . . and that,' said Brian. 'I
enjoyed it.'

And he and Dougal started to giggle like
anything.

'Tea, Dougal,' said Florence, sternly.

'May I have a spoon?' said Dougal,
screeching with laughter.

'Try a niblick,' said Brian, shrieking and
wiping his eyes on the cloth.

Uncle Hamish came in. They stopped
laughing very quickly.

'And what have you been doing, Uncle
Hamish?' said Florence.

Uncle Hamish looked at Dougal and Brian.

'I'd rather not talk about it,' he said, 'in
the present company.'

Highland Games

'Don't you think we've been here rather a long time?' said Florence, one day when they were all out for a walk. 'I don't want us to outstay our welcome.'

Everyone agreed that perhaps they should think of going back soon.

'We'll tell Uncle Hamish,' said Florence.

They told Uncle Hamish when they got back for lunch. He behaved rather strangely at the news. He got up and walked about, sniffed and sat down again.

'Ah, weel,' he said. 'Aye, aye, weel.'

Then he got up again and left without saying any more.

'Are all your relations like that?' said Brian.

'That's nothing,' said Dougal. 'You should

see my Auntie Megsie; she goes very funny
sometimes.'

'We must get him a present,' said
Florence, thoughtfully.

'Yes,' said Ermintrude. 'Very important.
He's been *sweet*.'

'But *what*?' said Mr Rusty.

They thought. Everything went quiet for a
very long time.

Mr MacHenry coughed.

'Yes?' they said.

'I was just coughing,' said Mr MacHenry.

'Oh,' they said.

They thought some more.

'You know what I think?' said Brian, suddenly.

'Yes, we do,' said Dougal.

'No, don't be rotten,' said Brian.

'Tell us, Brian,' said Florence.

'Well, I think he'd like us to feel that we appreciated Scotland, so I think we should give him a Highland Games.'

He looked round brightly.

'Do you know,' said Dougal, 'I think you may finally have had an idea.'

'Yes,' said Florence, 'he'd like that. We'll do him some Highland Games as a farewell present.'

So it was decided, and of course it was to be kept a secret from Uncle Hamish.

'Er . . . there's just one little thing,' said Mr Rusty.

'Yes?' they said.

'Er . . . what *are* Highland Games?' he asked.

They all looked at Brian.

'Well, they're . . . er . . . games,' he said, 'and they're played in the . . . er . . . Highlands.'

'What sort of games?' said Mr Rusty.

'Oh, all sorts,' said Brian.

'You are being vague and devious, snail,' said Dougal.

Ermintrude had a suggestion; they would ask Angus.

Angus was asked.

'Is it the Games ye're planning?' he said. 'The *Games*?'

'Yes, the Games,' they said.

'Oh, aye, I ken weel the Games,' said Angus.

'Perhaps you'd be kind enough to explain them to us?' they said.

'Weel, 'tis a gathering,' said Angus. 'A *gathering* of athletic souls in brawny bodies . . . aye . . . that it is.'

'Could you explain a little more, Angus?' said Florence. 'What do they do?'

'Weel, they toss the caber,' said Angus, 'and they pitch the hammer and they bend the bawbee and they slither the shovel and they call the yowes to the knowes sometimes . . . if they've a mind.'

He paused reflectively.

'I was good at that,' he said.

'I shall toss the caber,' said Dougal. 'If I can find one.'

'I shall dance my Highland Fling,' said Florence. 'If I can learn it.'

'I shall play the bag-pipes,' said Dylan.
'If I can borrow some.'

Mr MacHenry said he would provide
floral tributes and decorations and Mr Rusty
said he would announce the events.

'And I shall do a sword-dance,' said
Ermintrude. 'If I can find some swords.'

'What about you?' said Dougal to Brian.

'I shall provide a surprise item,' said Brian.

'It would surprise me if you could *spell*
item,' said Dougal.

'You may mock,' said Brian, 'but just you
wait.'

The next few days were spent preparing.
Dougal asked Big John to provide him with a
caber and Big John said he couldn't get one
before the day of the Games.

'Don't worry,' said Dougal, loftily. 'I don't
need practice.'

The day of the Games arrived. After
breakfast Uncle Hamish was led out to the
chosen field and seated in a special chair
covered in flowers and bunting. All his
attempts to discover what was happening
were 'shushed' and he was given a cup of tea
and told to 'wait and see.'

Dylan came out on to the field, called
unnecessarily for silence and proceeded to

open the games by playing so powerfully on the bagpipes that Uncle Hamish was seen to wilt.

Florence was next. Mr Rusty laid some boards flat, Dylan played the pipes and Florence gave Uncle Hamish her Highland Fling.

At the end Uncle Hamish roared to Florence that it was well done and would she come and sit by him?

Florence did so.

'What's next?' said Uncle Hamish, and Mr Rusty announced Ermintrude.

'Sword-dance,' whispered Florence.

'Oh, aye?' whispered Uncle Hamish.

Ermintrude hadn't been able to find any swords, so she laid a toasting fork and an old golf club on the dancing board Florence had used.

'Sword-dance,' she said proudly, stepping on and disappearing.

'Where's she gone?' said Uncle Hamish.

'I think the board broke,' said Florence, faintly. 'It must have been over a hole.'

Ermintrude's head appeared.

'Who put this board over a hole?' she said.

Mr Rusty confessed.

'It seemed a good idea at the time,' he

said. 'In case anyone fell in.'
'Someone *did*,'
said Ermintrude,
'but the show must go on.'
And she performed her
sword-dance to great acclaim.
– especially from Angus.

Mr Rusty announced Dougal.
'Caber tossing,' whispered Florence.
'Oh, aye?' whispered Uncle Hamish.
Dougal stepped into the middle of the arena.

'Big John,' he called. 'I'll trouble you for the caber.'

Big John ambled on pulling after him a tree-trunk of prodigious length and girth.

Dougal paled.

'What's that?' he asked.

'That's your caber,' said Big John.

'That's not a caber,' said Dougal, 'that's a *tree*.'

'A *small* tree,' said Big John, 'called a caber. You pick it up and throw it.'

'Pick it up and throw it?!' said Dougal, aghast.

'That's the general idea,' said Big John.

'I'm not sure the RSPCA would let me,' said Dougal.

He looked round. The Games field was full of expectant faces.

'I must be mad,' he groaned, and he got his shoulders under the caber and started to heave.

'Careful, Dougal!' called Florence.

'Now she tells me,' gritted Dougal, doing little runs backwards and forwards with the caber pointing straight up.

'Right, you've got it!' shouted Brian. 'Toss it forward.'

Dougal tried. The caber tilted. Everyone

gasped. The caber tilted more and Dougal set off at a run down the field.

'Throw it,' they shouted.

'I can't,' screeched Dougal.

'Let go,' they shouted.

'I can't!' screamed Dougal. 'It's caught in me kilt!'

He was gathering more speed, and as they watched he finally disappeared with a last little wail through a hole in the wall at the end of the field.

'He'll likely end up in Fife,' said Uncle Hamish.

There was a faint crash from the distance, and with a loud squawk Dougal flew back over into the field and landed in the middle with a bump.

'Are you all right, Dougal?' called Florence, anxiously.

Dougal got up and put his kilt straight.

'I have just,' he said slowly, 'run fourteen miles holding a tree. I have hit a rock and been flung back like a dob of mud into the middle of a field. OF COURSE I AM NOT ALL RIGHT!!'

'I don't think you got the principle of the thing quite right, old mate,' said Brian.

Dougal turned slowly and advanced on him.

'Why are you advancing on me like that?' said Brian, nervously.

'Because I am going to bury your head in the mud and laugh a lot,' said Dougal.

'But it's time for my surprise,' said Brian,

'Time for Brian's surprise!' they all shouted.

'Mollusc,' said Dougal, 'this had better be good.'

Mr Rusty called for silence. Brian went to the middle of the field, bowed right, left and centre and let out a piercing whistle.

There was a rushing of wings and hundreds
of pigeons flew low over the field, circled and
went high into the sky. With a bang a hole
opened in the field and thousands of balloons
floated up. The pigeons swooped down,
caught the balloons and swooped up again

high into the air. They let them go against
the blue sky and the balloons danced together
and formed the words . . .

The air filled with the sound of a thousand
pipers playing Uncle Hamish's favourite
tunes and with a PING and a BONG a table
appeared covered with a huge tea, with a
vast cake in the shape of a letter H.

'Brian!' breathed Florence. 'What a
surprise. How *did* you do it?'

Brian smiled modestly.

'I had a little help,' he said, and there was
Zebedee bonging around the middle of the
field laughing like anything.

'Zebedee, of course,' said Florence.

Uncle Hamish was very moved.

'It's been a great day,' he said, 'and it's
been great having ye here. Ye must come again.'

'Aye, haste ye back,' said Angus.

'We will,' they said.

The next morning after they'd all packed

and had a last look round, the train was found fast asleep in a siding and everyone loaded in.

'Oh, are we going back already?' said the train, yawning.

Florence looked at the hills and the trees.

'It's time to go,' she said, sadly.

Uncle Hamish and Angus and Big John packed provisions into the train and stood on the platform to wave goodbye.

'I may cry,' said Brian.

'Don't be so soft,' said Dougal, sniffing.

Uncle Hamish blew up his bagpipes and started to play a long sad tune.

'I *shall* cry,' said Brian.

'Got a hanky?' said Dougal.

'There's always next year,' said Zebedee, and the train gave a little toot.

They all brightened.

'It's April in the garden,' said Mr MacHenry, thoughtfully.

It was time to go.

So they went.